A LEGACY OF KNOWLEDGE
ACPL

Thailand

Donna Bailey

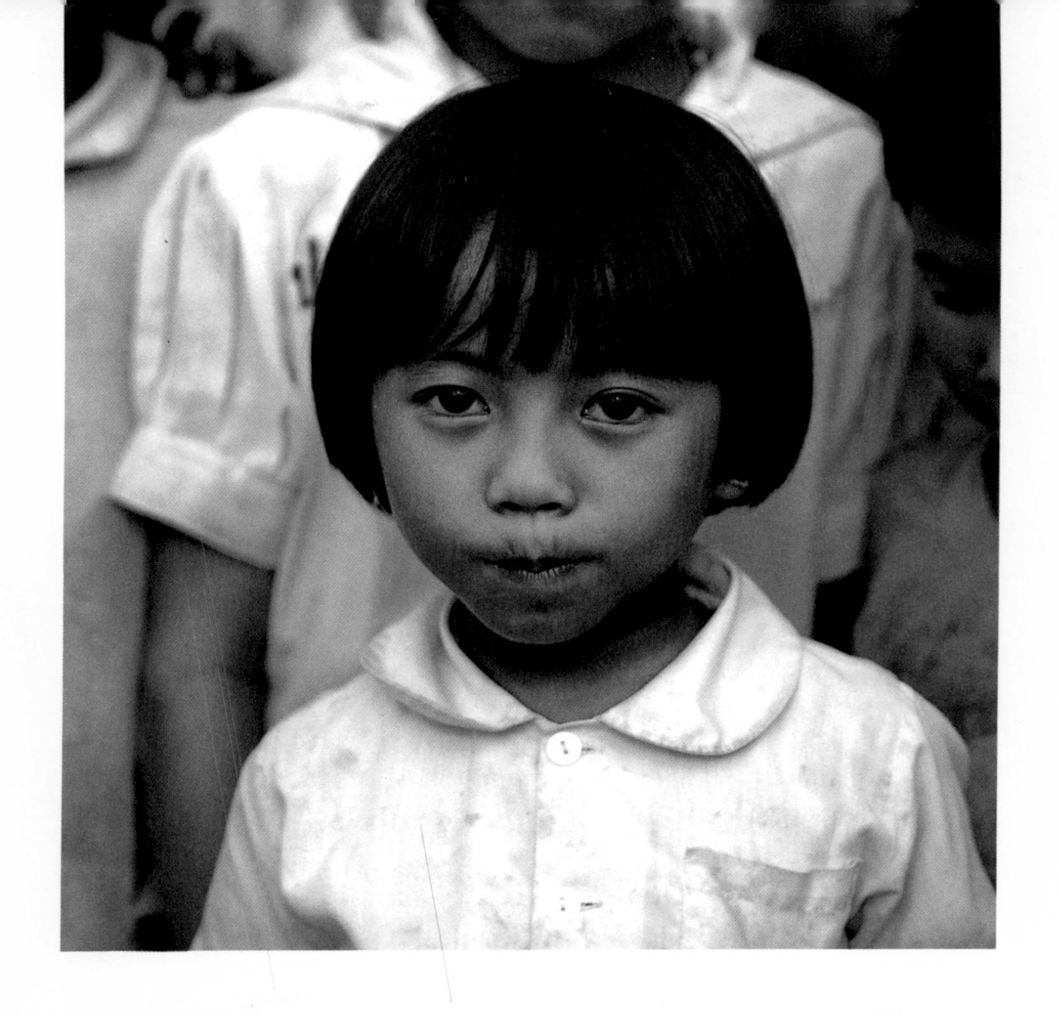

Hello! My name is Chula.
I live in the city of Bangkok.
Bangkok is the capital of Thailand.
The summer weather in Bangkok
is very hot and sticky.

The Chao Phraya River flows through the center of Bangkok.
There are many temples near the river.
Temples in Thailand are called wats.
Wat Arun, one of the biggest temples in Bangkok, is 250 feet tall.

Bangkok is a large, bustling city with
many cars, buses, and taxis.
Sometimes there are big
traffic jams, too!

One of the best ways to get around
Bangkok is in a tuk-tuk.
A tuk-tuk is a little three-wheeled taxi
that can dodge in and out of traffic.

In the wet season, especially in September, it rains very hard. The streets in Bangkok often flood as the river rises.

Bangkok has many canals called klongs.
Our house is built on a klong.
Houses like ours are built on
stilts so that water will not
get into the house during a flood.

People living along the banks of a klong
sometimes use boats instead of cars.
My friends and I go to school
by boat.

School starts at 8:30 in the morning.
At school we wear a uniform.
Everyone wears a white shirt.
The boys wear blue pants and
the girls wear blue skirts.

Our school day ends at
about 3:30 in the afternoon.
When I get home, my friends and
I often go swimming in the klong.
Swimming keeps us cool in the hot weather.

Sometimes I go with Mom to the market.
On the way, we often buy a snack at
a roadside stand.
We choose our food and the women
cook it while we wait.

Sometimes we go to the fruit and
vegetable market.
Mom buys lots of chilies because
Thai people like hot, spicy food.

Mom often goes to the floating market
to buy fish for supper.
Thai people eat a lot of
fresh fish and vegetables.

Mom makes many different
stews and salads.
For supper we often have
my favorite meal of fish and rice.
We eat rice with almost every meal.

On the weekend, we often visit
one of the nearby temples.
We cross the river on a motorboat
called a long-tail.

Mom takes food to the monks
who live in the temple.
We say prayers in front of the statue of
Buddha and leave offerings of
candles, fruit, and flowers.

Sometimes we go to the park to
fly kites.
In April there is an international
kite-flying festival.
People come to Thailand from all over
the world to take part in the festival.

There are many festivals in Thailand, especially in Chiang-Mai.
Chiang-Mai is in northern Thailand.
In February, when many kinds of flowers are in bloom, the people of Chiang-Mai have a flower festival.

Girls in colorful costumes ride on
floats covered with flowers.
The floats move in a procession through
the center of Chiang-Mai.

Musicians march in the parade and
play music for the dancers.
The musicians even have flowers
on their hat and their instrument.

These girls are also in the festival parade.
They are doing a special dance
from their region.

Girls from different regions of
northern Thailand wear their
traditional clothes in the parade.
The pants of these Yao girls are made
from cloth woven into special patterns.

Many traditional dresses have
embroidery on the skirts.
This girl wears a special headdress, too.

The Meo people wear clothes decorated with embroidery.
The little girls wear embroidered skirts and the boys have embroidered jackets.

Even very young Meo children learn to do embroidery.

People in the villages near Chiang-Mai
are skilled in many other handicrafts.
This silversmith is making a pattern
on a silver bowl.

These woodcarvers in the village of Bor Sang carve intricate patterns on furniture.

Bor Sang is also famous for
its handmade umbrellas.
First the workers make the frames
for the umbrellas.

After covering the frames with paper, the workers decorate the umbrellas with colorful patterns.

During the Umbrella Fair in January,
girls walk along the main street
carrying their umbrellas.
One of the girls is chosen
to be Miss Bor Sang.

Musicians and drummers also
take part in the parade.
These musicians have even
decorated their drum.

Acrobats show their skills during
the festival.
Crowds gather to watch the performers.

Index

Editorial Consultant: Donna Bailey
Executive Editor: Elizabeth Strauss
Project Editor: Becky Ward

Picture research by Jennifer Garratt
Designed by Richard Garratt Design

Photographs
Cover: Spectrum Colour Library
Hutchison: title page (Juliet Highel-Brimah), 2, 9 (Nancy Durrell McKenna), 5, 11, 12, 17 (Liba Taylor), 7, 8, 10 (Michael MacIntyre), 15 (Tim Motion), 27, 29 (R. Ian Lloyd), 28 (Christine Pemberton), 16
Insight Picture Library: 14 (J. Gearing)
Spectrum Colour Library: 18, 22, 23 (Jean Kugler), 19, 20, 21, 26, 30, 31, 32
Zefa: 3, 4, 6, 13, 24, 25

Library of Congress Cataloging-in-Publication Data: Bailey, Donna. Thailand/written by Donna Bailey. p. cm.—(Where we live) Includes index. SUMMARY: Describes life in Bangkok, the capital of Thailand. ISBN 0-8114-2570-3 1. Bangkok (Thailand)—Social life and customs—Juvenile literature. [1. Thailand—Social life and customs. 2. Bangkok (Thailand)—Social life and customs.] I. Title. II. Series: Bailey, Donna. Where we live. DS589.B2B35 1991 9593—dc20 91-22044 CIP AC

ISBN 0-8114-2570-3

1 2 3 4 5 6 7 8 9 0 LB 97 96 95 94 93 92